BY TOM ANGLEBERGER

Insp
Flyt

Amulet Books
New York

ILLUSTRATED BY CECE BELL

ctor

#2

rap

**THE PRESIDENT'S
MANE IS MISSING**

Library of Congress Cataloging-in-Publication Data

Angleberger, Tom, author.
Inspector Flytrap in The president's mane is missing! and other thrilling mysteries, co-starring Nina the Goat / by Tom Angleberger ; illustrated by Cece Bell.
pages cm
ISBN 978-1-4197-0955-5
[1. Mystery and detective stories. 2. Venus's flytrap—Fiction. 3. Goats—Fiction. 4. Animals—Fiction. 5. Humorous stories.] I. Bell, Cece, illustrator. II. Title. III. Title: President's mane is missing and other thrilling mysteries.
PZ7.A585Inw 2016
[Fic]—dc23
2015016399

Hardcover ISBN: 978-1-4197-0955-5
Paperback ISBN: 978-1-4197-0966-1

Text copyright © 2016 Tom Angleberger
Illustrations copyright © 2016 Cece Bell
Book design by Maria T. Middleton

Printed and bound in U.S.A.
10 9 8 7 6 5 4 3 2 1

Amulet Books are available at special discounts when purchased in quantity for premiums and promotions as well as fundraising or educational use. Special editions can also be created to specification. For details, contact specialsales@abramsbooks.com or the address below.

ABRAMS The Art of Books
115 West 18th Street, New York, NY 10011
abramsbooks.com

To illustration genius
Kyle T. Webster—thanks for
creating all those awesome
brushes!

CONTENTS

PART 1

Inspector Flytrap
in
The President's
Mane Is Missing

Chapter 1

My phone rang.

"Hello," I said. "Flytrap Detective Agency."

A slow voice started asking me questions.

"Is this . . . Mr. Flytrap?"

"My name," I answered, "is INSPECTOR Flytrap. I am a detective. Do you have a THRILLING mystery for me to solve?"

"Wait a minute," said the slow voice slowly. "I thought . . . you solved . . . BIG DEAL mysteries."

"Yes, I do," I said. "However, I am also trying to become the World's Greatest Detective. So I've decided to solve only THRILLING mysteries."

"But I have a . . . BIG DEAL mystery," said the slow voice.

"That's fine," I said, "as long as it is also THRILLING. Please tell me what the mystery is AS QUICKLY AS POSSIBLE, and I'll tell you if I am thrilled."

"I have lost my . . . pickle paperweight."

"I am NOT thrilled," I said. "A missing pickle paperweight is not THRILLING, and it's not even a BIG DEAL. Also, I have already found your pickle paperweight once before. Remember?"

"No . . . you found A pickle paperweight . . . but it was not MY pickle . . . paperweight."

"It wasn't?"

"No . . . mine is much bigger."

"How big is it?"

"Big enough for . . . a hoofed mammal to hide behind!"

"Well, that is big," I said. "But like I said, I solve only THRILLING mysteries!"

BIG
pickle
paperweight →

Misty →

And I hung up before he could start a slow argument about it!

Sheesh! I'm trying to become the greatest detective that ever grew! I don't have time to go around looking for big metal pickles!

Boop!

Chapter 2

y phone rang.

"Hello," I said. "Flytrap Detective Agency."

A rude voice started asking me questions.

"Is this Mr. Spyflap?"

"My name," I answered, "is Inspector Flytrap. I am a—

"What the hay is a flytrap?"

"A flytrap is a plant that eats flies."

"So your name is Spyflap the Flytrap?"

"It's not SPYFLAP," I yelled into the phone. "It's FLYTRAP!"

"That's nuts!"

"It's not nuts! I'm a Venus flytrap, so it makes sense that my name is Flytrap!"

"Yeah, maybe. But I still think Flytrap is a dumb name!"

"My name is *Inspector* Flytrap! I am a famous detective."

"Oh yeah? If you're so famous, how come I've never heard of you?"

"You must have heard of me!"

"Nope."

"But YOU are calling ME on the phone!"

"Well, I'm trying to reach Nina the Goat."

Nina the Goat is my assistant. Since I am a plant and live in a flowerpot, I need someone to move me from one thrilling crime scene to the next. Nina pushes me from place to place on a skateboard— really fast. Too fast!

"I'm sorry, Nina the Goat cannot talk on the phone right now."

"Why not?"

"Because if I give her the phone, she'll eat it."

"She still eats stuff?"

"Yes, she eats just about everything, including cans, can openers, wires, belt buckles, books, e-books, small cars, door-stops, lacrosse sticks, tables, and toilets."

"She ate the toilet?"

"Yes."

"How do you go to the bathroom?"

"I'm a plant. I don't have to go to the bathroom."

"Really? What about—"

"This is ridiculous!" I screamed into the phone. "My bathroom habits are none of your business! Now, do you want to leave a message for Nina or not?"

"Oh yeah ... uh ... tell her the President of the United States of America called. Just tell her to stop by the Capitol Building at noon. You can come, too, Flyball."

And then he hung up.

Chapter 3

Nina!" I shouted. "You won't believe this! The President of the United States just called you!'

"Big deal," replied Nina, chewing on the handle of my brand-new magnifying glass.

Nina rarely gets excited, but I thought she would show more interest than this.

"Nina, it was *the President of the United States*! President Horse G. Horse himself!"

"Did he leave a message?"

I handed her the message.

She ate it.

Luckily, I remembered what it said.

"Nina, he invited you to the Capitol Building today at noon!"

"Big deal."

"But it IS a big deal! Look at this newspaper! It says the President is going to make a thrilling announcement today at noon at the Capitol Building!"

She ate the newspaper.

Chapter 4

Nina pushed my skateboard across town to the Capitol Building.

There were lots of TV news reporters heading the same way. I hate big crowds! When you are a plant, you have to be extra-careful not to get stepped on.

"Excuse me," said a turkey. "I'm a TV news reporter. Are you thrilled about the President's big news?"

"Yes! I always read the news and—"

"Excuse me," interrupted the turkey. "I was talking to the goat."

"Oh," I said.

"No comment," said Nina.

The turkey gave up and started interviewing a nearby sloth, who was eating a hot dog.

At last we were coming up to the Capitol Building. But we could barely see it.

There was something huge in front of it. Bigger than the building! But no one could see what it was, because it was covered with a gigantic tarp.

"What is it?" the TV news reporters asked each other.

"I don't know. It's a mystery!" they replied.

"AHA!" I shouted to get their attention. "I, Inspector Flytrap, have solved the mystery! The President is going to take off the tarp, and we will see that it is a big statue, probably of a thrilling figure from U.S. history, like George Washington or Harriet Tubman."

Just then a rude voice came booming at us from big speakers.

"Everyone be quiet! It's my turn to talk! This is President Horse G. Horse and— HEY! I said HUSH IT UP! And look over here! Eyes on me!"

We all turned to where the President was standing on the Capitol steps.

"OK, that's better! So I'm here to remove the tarp so you can see this big statue of a thrilling figure from U.S. history."

"See? I was right!" I said, but none of the TV news reporters were listening and Nina had disappeared.

The President pushed a button, and the tarp dropped.

It was a statue of President Horse G. Horse.

Chapter 5

I will now answer questions from the reporters about this thrilling new statue of me, President Horse G. Horse, which was created by the famous artist Vanessa Cowcow."

Nobody had any questions.

"OK . . . I will also answer questions about my beautiful new presidential limousine! Isn't it awesome?"

Nobody had any questions.

"All right . . . I will also answer questions about my collection of salt and pepper shakers."

There was a long, awkward silence. Not a very thrilling silence, either.

Actually, it wasn't completely silent. There was a faraway sound . . . sort of a *munch, munch, munch* sound.

I looked around for Nina. I couldn't find her.

I thought about asking the President if he had seen her, but someone else was finally asking him a question.

"Excuse me!" shouted a TV news reporter. "Why doesn't the statue have a mane?"

"What?" snarled the President.

"A mane—you know, the long hair running down the back of your neck."

"I know what a mane is, you turkey! I'm a horse!"

"Well, then . . . why isn't there a mane on your statue?"

"What?" snarled the President again.

"Just look up!"

The President looked up.

"MY STATUE!" yelled the President.  "THE MANE IS MISSING! Call the Secret Service! Call the Marines! Call the FBI! Somebody figure out where my mane is!"

"AHA!" I yelled. "Mr. President, I can solve this THRILLING mystery for you!"

The President and all the TV news reporters turned to look at me.

"Who the hay are you?" the President asked.

"I'm Inspector Flytrap, the famous detective."

"Oh yeah? If you're so famous, how come I've never heard of you?"

"You HAVE heard of me! We talked on the phone this morning!"

"Oh yeah. Flyball—the guy who doesn't use the toilet," said the President.

All the TV news reporters started to gobble, "You don't use a toilet? Why don't

you use a toilet? Are you protesting toilets?"

"NO COMMENT!" I yelled.

"OK, Flyball," said the President. "Since you think you know everything, what happened to my mane?"

"My goat ate it," I said, and pointed up at the top of the statue, where we could see the distant form of Nina the Goat, now chewing away at the statue's ears.

"This is the second time she's broken my heart," groaned the president, bursting into tears.

Chapter 6

y phone rang.

"Hello," I said. "Flytrap Detective Agency."

A gobbly voice started talking to me.

"Mr. Flytrap, this is Greta Von Hopinstop with CNNNNNNM News. I just have one more question."

"My name is *Inspector* Flytrap, and I

will only answer questions that do NOT involve how I use the bathroom."

She hung up.

I sat there at my desk for a few minutes and watched Nina nibbling at my new file cabinet.

My phone rang.

"Hello," I said. "Flytrap Detective Agency."

A gobbly voice started talking to me.

"Mr. Flytrap, this is Greta Von Hopin-stop with CNNNNNNM News. I just have one more question, and it does not involve a toilet."

"OK," I said. "What is it?"

"How did Nina the Goat get up on top of that huge statue, anyway?"

I realized that I hadn't solved that part of the mystery yet.

"Just a moment," I told Greta, putting a leaf over the phone.

"Pssst! Nina!" I whispered. "How did you get up on top of that statue in the first place?"

"Elevator."

"What? I didn't see one. Where was it?"

"In his butt."

"Ahem," I said, taking my leaf off the phone. "Greta, I think that should remain a mystery."

THIS WAY TO ELEVATOR TO THE GLORIOUS PRESIDENTIAL STATUE

THE HORSE'S CENSORED!!

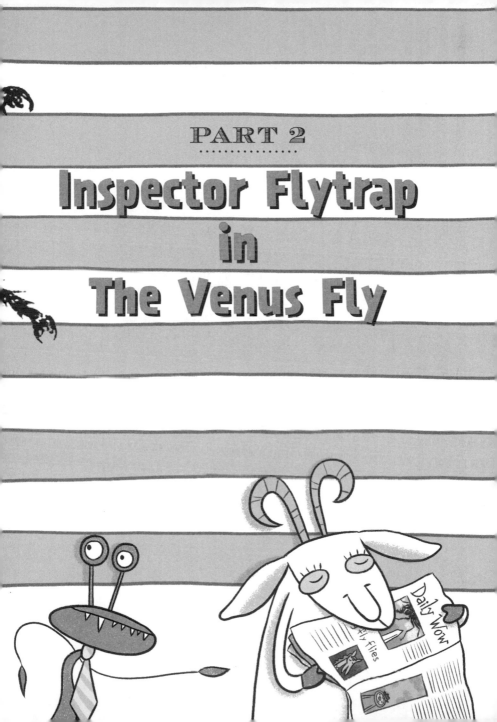

PART 2

Inspector Flytrap
in
The Venus Fly

Chapter 7

My phone rang.

"Hello," I said. "Flytrap Detective Agency."

"Is this Inspector Flytrap, the most handsome detective that ever grew?"

It was Wanda, the most beautiful rose in the world!

"Wanda!" I shouted. "Oh, darling, it is so nice to talk to you!"

"BLEERPH," said Nina, and she began choking.

"It is nice to talk to you, too," Wanda said. "I was calling to see if we could have a date tonight."

"Oh boy!" I said.

"BLARRRK!" said Nina, and she began gagging.

"Wonderful!" I said. "I'll call Penguini's Linguini and get a romantic table for two."

"AHEM!" said Nina, and she began stamping her hoof.

"Er . . . ," I said, "Nina wants to know if William can join us?"

William is the goat who pushes Wanda's flowerpot around on a skateboard.

"Yes," said Wanda. "So make it a table

for four. Bye, darling. See you tonight!"

I was so happy!

"I just hope no THRILLING NATIONAL EMERGENCY happens that might make me miss the date," I said.

"Me, too," said Nina. "I want to do a lot of kissing tonight."

Chapter 8

y phone rang.

"Flytrap Detective Agency," I said. "Do you have a THRILL-ING mystery for me to solve?"

"Could I speak to Mr. Claptrap?" said a rude voice.

It was President Horse G. Horse again.

"My name is *Inspector* Fly-TRAP!"

"Oh yeah. Whatever. Listen, pal, I have

a national emergency here."

"Sorry, I solve mysteries, not national emergencies."

"Your country needs you!"

"Well," I said, "maybe if it's a THRILL-ING national emergency. Is it a THRILL-ING national emergency?"

"Yes."

"You're sure?" I asked. "I've been fooled before by people who think they have a

Buzz-buzz!

THRILLING national emergency, and then it turns out to be something like a pesky fly buzzing around."

"Yes, I'm sure."

"Okay, what is the THRILLING national emergency?"

"There's a pesky fly buzzing around."

"I'm sorry, Mr. President, that is a tasty snack, not a thrilling national emergency. Goodbye."

I hung up.

CLICK!

Chapter 9

y phone rang.

"How dare you hang up on the President of the United States!" shouted an angry voice.

"Who is this?"

"This is the President's mom. You've made him cry."

"I'm sorry."

"He's so upset, his mane is falling out!"

"I'm sorry. If you put him on the phone, I'll apologize."

The President got back on the phone.

"Mr. President, I am very sorry."

"Thank you, Claptrap. I accept your apology."

"My name is—"

"Now, if you'll close your big leafy mouth for a minute, I've got something to tell you about this fly."

"OK," I said.

"Are you sitting down?"

"I am a plant," I said. "I don't sit down."

"Then how do you—

Oh, never mind. Here's what I forgot to tell you: The pesky fly is 400 feet tall!"

"WHAT?" I shrieked.

"Yes! It's a alien space fly from another planet, and it's buzzing around the city and scaring everyone!"

"You mean it's a ..."

"Yes! It's a VENUS FLY!" shouted the president. "And since you're a Venus fly-TRAP, you're our only hope!"

"Sir, it will be an honor to serve my country and solve this THRILLING—"

"JUST GET RID OF THE FLY!"

He hung up.

Chapter 10

Nina! We've got to go! There's a THRILLING national emergency! A 400-foot-tall Venus fly is attacking the city."

"Big deal."

"It IS a big deal, Nina! Look—there it goes now!"

We looked out the window.

A giant fly was swooping over the city,

causing panic, riots, traffic jams, and undue delays.

"That buzzing is *really* annoying," said Nina, putting on a pair of earmuffs.

"That's why we've got to do something about it!"

"What?"

"I said, 'That's why we've got to do something about it!'"

"I heard your loud, grating voice through the earmuffs," said Nina, rolling her eyes. "I meant: WHAT are you going to do about it?"

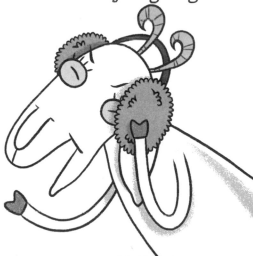

"Uh . . . ," I started, but I didn't know what to say next. What *could* we do about a 400-foot-tall fly? I know everything about normal-size flies but nothing about giant ones. I needed information!

"Nina, hand me volume *F* of the encyclopedia so I can look up 'Flies'!"

"Ate it."

"Nina! How could you? OK, hand me volume G so I can look up 'Giant Flies'!"

"Ate it."

"NINA! Those were expensive! How about volume V for 'Venus Flies'?"

"Ate it."

"*I* for 'Insects'?"

"Ate it."

"*B* for 'Bugs'?"

"Ate it."

"Uh . . . *M* for '*Musca domestica*,' the scientific name of the housefly?"

"Drank it."

"Drank it? How could you drink a volume of the encyclopedia?"

"Mmm . . . book smoothie!"

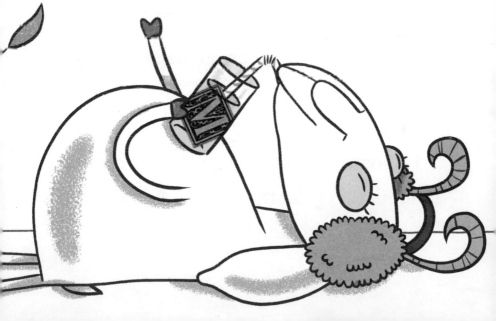

"This is ridiculous! Is there ANY volume left?"

"Page 57 of the *P* volume."

"All right, let me see it."

She handed me the single page.

The pig, or common swine, is one of the smartest of all animals. In fact, some scholars think pigs may have invented the wheel.

Pigs enjoy science, the arts, and mud. They eat a variety of foods, including beans, lasagna, and choice baked goods. They live all over the world, preferring farms to cities, and sometimes wear clothes during the holidays.

"Pig," I read. "The pig, or common swine, is one of the smartest of all animals. In fact, some scholars think pigs may have invented the—"

Nina ate page 57.

"Hmm," I murmured thoughtfully. "If pigs are so smart, maybe I should ask some pigs for information about this giant fly disaster. But where am I supposed to find a bunch of pigs?"

Chapter 11

My phone rang.

"Hello," I said. "Flytrap Detective Agency. Inspector Flytrap speaking."

"Oink," said a smart voice.

"Are you a pig?" I asked.

"Yes," she said.

"Are you one of those smart pigs?"

"Yes."

"How smart are you?"

"I'm the president of the National Science Headquarters."

"Wow! Could you guys help me save the city from destruction by giving me information about the giant fly from Venus?"

"Sure. Come right over."

"Great, we'll be right there."

"OK," said the smart voice. "See you later."

"Just a second," I said. "You were the one who called me. Did you want something?"

"Actually, I must have dialed the wrong number. I was trying to order a pizza."

She hung up.

"Nina, Let's go!" I shouted. "Get me

to the National Science Headquarters, so our nation's greatest thinkers can help us solve this THRILLING national emergency."

"Could we stop at a bookstore on the way?" asked Nina. "It's almost lunchtime."

Chapter 12

Nina pushed me out the door, and we hailed a taxi.

"Quick!" I ordered. "Take us to the National Science Headquarters, so we can get help from our nation's greatest thinkers."

"I can't," said the cabbie, who by the way was a donkey.

"Why not?"

"Your goat just ate the steering wheel."

We hailed ANOTHER taxi!

"Quick!" I ordered. "While carefully protecting the steering wheel, gearshift, and other important car parts, take us to the National Science Headquarters, so we can get help from our nation's greatest thinkers."

"OK," said the cabbie. He drove about thirty feet and stopped.

"What's the problem?" I demanded.

"We're there," said the cabbie, who by the way was a mule.

Oops. I had forgotten the National Science Headquarters is right next door to my office.

"That'll be fifty bucks," said the mule.

"Yeah, and two hundred bucks to replace my steering wheel!" shouted the donkey from thirty feet away.

Suddenly the buzzing sound got louder. The giant alien space fly was coming right for us. Two of its massive legs—each as big as a telephone pole—reached down and grabbed the two taxicabs.

Luckily, Nina pushed us out the door just as the fly was taking off with the taxis.

Clatter! went my skateboard onto the sidewalk. *Thud! Oof!* went me and my flowerpot onto the sidewalk. *Spluff* . . . went Nina as she landed softly on a nearby sloth, who was eating a hot dog.

Nina helped get me and my flower-pot back on the skateboard, and then she began eating a sign that said NATIONAL SCIENCE HEADQUARTERS—RING BELL IN CASE OF THRILLING NATIONAL EMERGENCY.

"No time for that now, Nina!" I yelled, pushing the doorbell button. "We've got to get inside and solve this case before the giant Venus fly strikes again."

"Pig deal," she said.

I saw that the door was open and twenty-three pigs in lab coats were waiting for us.

Chapter 13

INA!" yelled all twenty-three pigs, and they rushed forward to hug her.

"Ahem...," I said.

Nina took off her earmuffs and they all began chattering away about celebrity gossip, nuclear physics, and hoof care products. Why is Nina always so popular? I'm the famous detective! And I don't go around eating things that don't belong to me unless they are flies. "This is not a hugging emergency. It's a THRILLING emergency! We need to solve this giant-fly problem."

"OK, go ahead, solve it," said the first pig.

"Yeah, we're waiting," said the second pig.

"Well, I don't have a solution yet!" I snapped. "That's why I'm here! I need some scientific information about the giant alien space fly."

"Well, first of all, it's big," said the third pig.

"I already knew that," I said.

"REALLY big," said the fourth pig.

"REALLY REALLLLLLLLY BIG," said the fifth pig.

"We've never seen anything like it before!" said the sixth pig.

"Well, actually, we've seen lots of flies like this before," said the seventh pig.

"Just smaller," said the eighth pig.

"We've used the Computatotron 80001 to pinpoint every sighting of the giant Venus fly on this map," said the ninth pig,

RING BELL FOR SERVICE

COMPUTATOTRON 80001

```
10 CONSOLE 0,25,0,1:CLS 3
20 FOR I=1 TO
30 X=INT(RND(1)*640)
40 Y=INT(RND(1)*200)
50 CIRCLE(X,Y),50,I
60 PAINT(X,Y),I,I
70 NEXT
```

Ok

go to

pulling a map from the computer's printer.

"Could you please ask your goat not to eat the map?" said the tenth pig.

"Thank you," said the eleventh pig.

"As you can see, the giant fly is basically flying in circles around the city," said the twelfth pig.

"That wouldn't be such a problem if it wasn't destroying national landmarks every time it lands," said the thirteenth pig.

BUZZZZZ . . . CRACK . . . CRASH! came a terrible noise from outside.

The fourteenth pig wet his pants.

"That was the Washington Monument!" said the fifteenth pig.

"But why is he doing this?" said the sixteenth pig.

"WHY? WHY? WHY? WHY?" squealed the seventeenth, eighteenth, nineteenth, and twentieth pigs together.

"Big squeal," said Nina, and she put her earmuffs back on.

"Brilliant!" I said.

"Really? Which one of us was brilliant?" asked all the pigs together.

"The ones who asked Why? Why? Why? Why?"

"Why?"

"Yes, that is the correct question. I have been asking the wrong question. If you ask the wrong question, you'll never get the right answer. And if you never get the right answer, you'll never be the World's Greatest Detective."

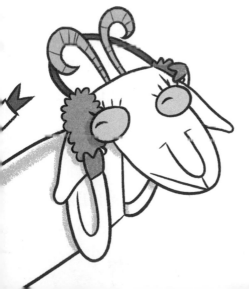

"None of us wants to be the World's Greatest Detective," said the pigs.

"But I do!" I said. "And that's why I am now going to ask the right question: 'Why is the fly doing this?' If we can answer that question, then we'll know how to stop it."

All the pigs squealed with excitement.

"So tell us why, already," said Nina.

"Er . . . I don't actually know why."

All the pigs grumbled with disappointment.

"But I know how to find out!"

All the pigs squealed with excitement. But I have to admit they didn't squeal as loud as they had before, and a couple of them left to check their email.

"To solve a crime, one must think like a

criminal," I told the pigs. "So in this case it will be necessary for me to think like a fly."

I thought like a fly.

"AHA!" I shouted. "I have solved this THRILLING mystery!"

"You have?" asked the twenty-first pig.

"By thinking like a fly?" asked the twenty-second pig.

"Yes!" I said! "What is different about this city today? What is here now that wasn't here yesterday?"

"A statue of President Horse G. Horse, with most of the mane missing?" said the twenty-third pig.

"Yes!" I said. "Now, think about it from the giant fly's point of view. He sees a horse . . . the biggest horse he's ever seen

". . . a horse bigger than the Capitol Building! So what does he think?"

No one said anything, so I told them.

"Every fly—big or small—knows one thing: Where there's a horse, there is horse poop! And flies sure do love horse poop! Since a regular-size horse makes a regular-size poop, this giant alien space fly is waiting for this giant horse to make a giant poop so it can have a giant lunch!"

"Speaking of lunch . . . ," said Nina.

"Not now, Nina," I said. "We've got to tell the President to tear down the statue before the giant Venus fly destroys Washington, America, life, liberty, and the pursuit of happiness!"

PART 3

Inspector Flytrap Has Lunch

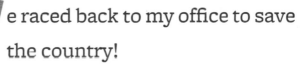

Chapter 14

We raced back to my office to save the country!

But then I heard something— a buzzing sound.

"Nina, STOP!" I yelled.

Nina stopped. Unfortunately, I kept rolling!

SLAM! I crashed right into a trash can.

Now the buzzing sound was REALLY loud.

But it wasn't the scary buzzing sound of one gigantic alien space fly. It was the beautiful buzzing sound of about a dozen regular-size flies. Mmmm!

"Inspector! Welcome!" called a familiar voice.

"Penguini!" I cried. "It is great to see you! But what are you doing here? Your restaurant is on the other side of town."

"Yes," said Penguini. "But this is my new food truck. Now I can serve food anywhere in the city!"

"Wonderful!" I cried. "Now I can eat the flies that hover around your garbage cans anywhere in the city!"

"Yes," said Penguini, "and your goat may eat as much of the garbage as she wants."

"Blurp," said Nina, who had already eaten ALL of the garbage. "Don't forget about supper," she added.

"Ah, yes! Penguini, we need to make a reservation at your restaurant tonight!"

"A date with that beautiful rose?" he asked.

"Yes," I said.

"Ahem," said Nina.

". . . and two goats," I said.

"Very good!" said Penguini. "I'll see you there tonight!"

BLURP!

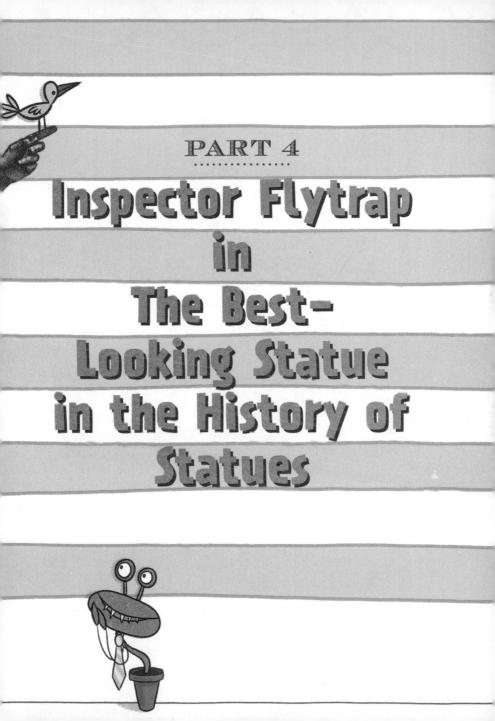

PART 4

Inspector Flytrap in The Best-Looking Statue in the History of Statues

Chapter 15

The President's phone rang.

"Hello," he said in a rude voice.

"This is Inspector Flytrap! I've solved the mystery. The giant fly is attracted to the giant statue of you because it thinks a giant pile of horse poop is going to come out. But since it's a statue, that won't happen, so the fly will just keep buzzing around until it destroys the whole city, the whole country, the whole world!"

"NEVER!" said the President. "Isn't there some way to stop it?"

"Yes, there is! I, Inspector Flytrap, have the answer! Mr. President, for the sake of the city, for the country, for the world . . . tear down that statue!"

"Nope," he said.

"WHAT?"

"Nope. You'll just have to find another way. The statue stays."

"BUT—"

"I said *Nope*, you stupid plant. And I'm the President, so you can't make me! So HA-HA! So find some other way to save the city, the country, and the world. I'll be busy taking photos of myself holding my

salt and pepper shakers next to my limo
parked under my statue of me! Say hi to
Nina!"

He hung up.

Chapter 16

f science can't help solve this THRILL-
ING national emergency," I said to
myself, "that leaves art. But how can
art help us now?"

That's when I realized it was the skill
and vision of an artist that had created a
horse statue so lifelike it fooled the giant
fly. Perhaps . . . perhaps that artist could
save us now.

"Quick, Nina! Take me to the studio of Vanessa Cowcow right now!"

"That rhymed," said Nina.

"Oh, sorry."

"I don't like rhymes," she said.

"I said I was sorry," I pleaded.

"You'd better be," she said.

Nina was grumpy and rude all the way to Vanessa Cowcow's studio, but she got me there without too much trouble.

"Vanessa Cowcow! Vanessa Cowcow!" I yelled, banging on the door with a leaf.

The door opened. A cow came out.

"Mmmm! Yummers! Lunch!" the cow said and tried to eat me!

Nina stepped in the way. No one was having lunch without her.

"NO! I'm not lunch! I'm Inspector Fly-trap, and I need your help to save the world!"

"Oh . . . OK. Come right in," she said.

I explained the problem.

"Since the President won't let us take the statue down, we need you to make a new, even bigger statue that will make the fly go away."

"A bigger statue? OK . . . but what will it be a statue of?"

"It needs to be the scariest thing in the world . . . to a fly."

"A spider?" she guessed.

"No, that would scare everybody else, too."

"A flyswatter?" she guessed.

"No, that would be ugly! We need something beautiful!"

"I give up," she said.

"Oh, come on . . . think . . . something that scares flies . . . but is also beautiful . . . or perhaps I should say handsome!"

"Oh no," groaned Vanessa Cowcow.

"Oh no," moaned Nina.

"Oh yes!" I exclaimed. "What we need is an enormous statue of . . . ME!"

Chapter 17

y phone rang. I was busy, so I let the caller leave a message on my voicemail.

"Hello, this is Inspector Flytrap. I can't answer the phone right now because I am posing for the famous artist Vanessa Cow-cow, who is sculpting a 500-foot-tall statue of me to ride on top of the statue of President Horse G. Horse."

Click.

"Flyslap! This is President Horse G. Horse! Tell Vanessa to hurry! The alien space fly has destroyed the Millard Fillmore Monument and the Supreme Court's Robe Depository. Worst of all, it's eaten the world's largest banana from the U.S. Botanical Garden!"

"Big peel," said Nina.

bricks!

marble!

egg cartons!

steel!

Chapter 18

For the next week, the giant alien space fly continued to fly above the city.

But the citizens were no longer helpless!

Oh, wait—they were *still* helpless, actually, when the giant fly swooped down to eat their cars, houses, bicycles, garages, and supermarkets.

But they weren't HOPELESS!

They all had hope now, because, soon, high above the city buildings, a giant statue of me would stand guard.

Following orders from Vanessa Cow-cow, whole herds of sheep were working to create the largest statue in America out of bricks, marble, steel beams, duct tape, and empty egg cartons.

Each day it grew by five or six stories. But no one could see it, because Vanessa Cow-cow insisted that it be kept under a tarp.

"Oh, Nina," I sighed. "Imagine how beautiful the city will look with this giant statue of me towering above it!"

Nina began hacking and gagging. Possibly she was choking on the linoleum floor she was eating.

SHEEP POWER!

Chapter 19

My phone rang.

"Flyclap! Get down here! Statue's ready!" yelled the very familiar, very rude voice of President Horse G. Horse.

"My name is—," I began.

But he had already hung up.

Nina pushed me down to the Capitol Building.

There was the enormous statue of President Horse G. Horse, and perched on its back was an even taller statue covered with an enormous tarp.

The whole area was packed with turkey news reporters, donkey congressmen, sheep sculptors, duck Secret Service agents, a sloth eating a hot dog, and nine geese in their underwear. (These were the Supreme Court Justices. You may recall that their Robe Depository had been destroyed.) Thousands and thousands of other animal citizens were there, too.

Nina pushed me up to the Capitol steps, where the President and Vanessa Cowcow were waiting.

"Hurry! Hurry! The alien space fly is

about to attack the White House! That's where I live!"

"OK . . . unveil the sculpture!" shouted Vanessa Cowcow, and a team of oxen began pulling on the ropes attached to the tarp. Finally it fell free, and the world's most amazingly beautiful statue was revealed.

It was me looking extremely brave. . . and, of course, handsome.

But would it work? Would it really scare

> Gag me with a spoon!
> That statue is SCARY!

away the giant alien space fly?

A loud roaring buzz gave us our answer! The mighty insect was zooming in close to get a good look!

Then the giant alien space fly made a thunderous hacking and gagging sound.

Then it turned skyward and zoomed away . . . up, up, up through the atmosphere and into space . . . leaving our planet in peace forever.

Chapter 20

The crowd let out a mighty cheer!

President Horse G. Horse hopped up and down, neighing, "You saved the White House! You saved my salt and pepper shaker collection! You saved my limo! Oh yeah—also the city, the country, and the world!"

"Speech! Speech!" the crowd began chanting.

"Ladies and gentlemen," President Horse G. Horse bellowed into the microphone. "Here is our thrilling national hero, FLYBLAP!"

President Horse G. Horse handed me the microphone, along with the Presidential Medal of Awesomeness. Dozens of cameras zoomed in for a close-up.

As I stood there on the steps of the Capitol Building looking out at the crowd, I realized my dream of being the Greatest Detective in the World had at last come true! Spread out before me were thousands and thousands of happy animals, all chanting my name. Where was Nina? I wanted her to see this!

"Flyblap! Flyblap! Flyblap!"

As I raised the microphone to my mouth, the crowd grew quiet. In the sudden silence, I thought I heard a distant *munch, munch, munch.*

Chapter 21

Then there was a really loud cracking sound above my head.

We all looked up. The statue of me had a big crack running right through the middle!

"NOOOOOOOOOOOO!" shouted President Horse G. Horse.

"NOOOOOOOOOOOOOOOOOO!" shouted Vanessa Cowcow.

"NOOOOOOOOOOOOOOOOOOOOOO!" shouted me.

The statue of me was toppling over! It had split in two, and the gargantuan—but handsome—likeness of my head was falling slowly to earth.

CRAHHHBASSHHHAKAAAWABLAH!

First it crushed the Capitol Building, then the art museum, the hospital, the fire station, the ice cream parlor, all remaining frozen yogurt stands, the mall, the videogame store, the videogame factory, a stadium where the greatest band in the world was giving a free concert, a playground with a really cool slide, the taco restaurant that makes the best tacos ever, and, lastly, the White House.

My statue was no more . . . and the nation's capital was in ruins.

"My shakers . . . my shakers," wailed the President. But then he looked around and smiled. "But at least my beautiful new presidential limousine is still OK."

Just then the statue of President Horse G. Horse broke in two. The enormous rear end of the giant horse fell backward

and crashed right on top of the presidential limousine. It landed so hard that the ground shook like we were having an earthquake.

Everyone was knocked down by the shockwave, and as they staggered to their feet, I could see that they weren't happy anymore! They weren't hushed anymore! They were furious!

"Get him!" They all roared in unison and surged toward the steps.

Luckily, I wasn't there anymore!

Chapter 22

The shockwave had started my skateboard rolling, then bouncing uncontrollably down the steps.

Desperately, I wrapped a vine around the board to keep from being thrown off. At the bottom of the steps, I landed on the street with a bounce, and because Capitol Hill is pretty steep, I kept on rolling and picking up speed.

I didn't know how I was going to stop. But I didn't want to stop! I just wanted to get away from the angry mob, which was now chasing me.

Leading the pack of furious donkeys, pigs, sheep, ducks, and nearly naked geese was the President himself, screaming, "Get him! Get Flyblap!"

Then I heard a whistling-munching sort of sound in the air. I looked up to see an animal falling out of the sky. It looked like it was going to fall right on top of me!

SPLAT!

It did fall right on top of me!

It was Nina! She was still chewing on a big chunk of my statue. I always knew she would eat me one day!

"Nina!" I scolded as we careened uncontrollably through the rubble-strewn streets of the half-ruined city. "You destroyed the Capitol, the White House, most of the city, my statue, and my reputation! I hope you're happy!"

"Not really," said Nina, spitting out a mouthful of statue. "You tasted terrible."

"That's hurtful," I said.

Behind us the screaming, yelling, and bleating were getting louder. The crowd was gaining on us.

"Nina! The President, the Congress, the Supreme Court, the Secret Service, the Army, the Navy, the Marines, the

QUE!?

Coast Guard, the Department of Agriculture, AND the TV news reporters are all chasing us! Even you can't outrun them

all! We've got to find somewhere to hide!"

"How about behind that very large metal pickle?" asked Nina.

Nina swerved the skateboard, and we crashed to a stop in the shadow of a giant pickle, just in time.

The President, the Congress, the Supreme Court, the Secret Service, the Army, the Navy, the Marines, the Coast Guard, the Department of Agriculture, AND the TV news reporters all rushed past.

"Aha," I whispered. "I just solved the mystery of the big, lost pickle paperweight."

"Big dill," said Nina.

Chapter 23

nspector Flytrap! Welcome!"

I looked up . . . Who could possibly be glad to see me?

It was Penguini!

"Please come around to the back," he said. "My restaurant has been destroyed, but my trash cans are still full of delicious trash . . . and flies! Your table is ready for you in the alley, and your beautiful date has just arrived."

My date! I had forgotten all about her!

"And Nina . . . your date is here, too!" said Penguini.

Nina pushed me around to the trash cans as fast as she could. A little too fast, really! I barely had time to straighten my tie and uncrumple my leaves.

Penguini poured some sparkling water into our pots, and Wanda and I gazed into each other's eyes. In the distance, the police, the President, the President's mom, and the entire United States military continued their search.

And we lived happily ever after.

ABOUT THE AUTHOR

TOM ANGLEBERGER is the author of the best-selling Origami Yoda series, as well as *Fake Mustache* and *Horton Halfpott*, both Edgar Award nominees, and the Qwikpick Papers series. Visit Tom online at origamiyoda.com.

"HONEST" TOM A.

CECE "WOODEN TEETH" BELL

ABOUT THE ILLUSTRATOR

CECE BELL is the author of the *New York Times* bestselling *El Deafo*, which won a Newbery Honor. She is also the author of *The Rabbit and Robot* books. Tom and Cece are married and live in Christiansburg, Virginia.